I Am A
Flower Girl

A Grosset & Dunlap ALL ABOARD BOOK®

To Victoria—W.C.L.

Special thanks to Ted, Jessie, and Katy
and to White's Catering
and to the Crosby Mansion.

Text copyright © 1999 by Wendy Cheyette Lewison. Photographs copyright © 1999 by Elizabeth Hathon. All rights reserved. Published by Grosset & Dunlap, Inc., a member of Penguin Putnam Books for Young Readers, New York. GROSSET & DUNLAP is a trademark of Grosset & Dunlap, Inc. ALL ABOARD BOOKS is a trademark of Grosset & Dunlap, Inc. Registered in U.S. Patent and Trademark Office. THE LITTLE ENGINE THAT COULD and engine design are trademarks Platt & Munk, Publishers, a division of Grosset & Dunlap, Inc. Published simultaneously in Canada. Printed in the U.S.A.

Library of Congress Cataloging-in-Publication Data
Lewison, Wendy Cheyette.
    I am a flower girl / by Wendy Cheyette Lewison ; photographs by Elizabeth Hathon.
        p.   cm. — (A Grosset & Dunlap all aboard book)
    Summary: Katy helps Aunt Jessica plan her wedding, at which Katy is to be the flower girl.
    [1. Weddings—Fiction. 2. Aunts—Fiction.] I. Hathon, Elizabeth, ill. II. Title. III. Series.
    PZ7.L5884Iac   1999
    [E]—dc21
                                                                    98-32219
                                                                    CIP
ISBN 0-448-41956-4   A B C D E F G H I J   AC

I Am A
Flower
Girl

By Wendy Cheyette Lewison

Photographs by
Elizabeth Hathon

Grosset & Dunlap, Publishers

My Aunt Jessica has great news. She's getting married!

She shows us her ring. "Look, Katy!" she says to me. "Look at the ring Ted gave me! Isn't it beautiful?"

Aunt Jessica wants everyone in the family to see her ring. She wants everyone in the *world* to see it! She is so happy!

There's more great news. I'm going to be a flower girl at the wedding! I want to practice being a flower girl right away.

I get my sand pail and make believe it's a pretty basket.

Then I pick some flowers from the garden, and put them in my pail.

Now I try walking—slowly, very slowly. How am I doing?

A flower girl has to look pretty, just like the bride. She has to wear a pretty dress, says my mom. So we go to the fancy dress store.

Mom tells me it will be fun to try them on.... But she knows I've never liked wearing dresses!

Mom starts picking out dresses. I don't think I'll like any of them.

"No! I just can't. I'm sure it'll *itch*!"

Well, I guess this one *is* pretty.... But it's too long.
I don't want to trip going down the aisle.

Now here is one I like!

All I need are the right shoes.

These pink ones are nice and comfortable. My outfit will be perfect! I can't wait for the big day to arrive.

The weeks pass by—slowly, very slowly. It's hard to wait.

Then all of a sudden, Mom says the wedding is tomorrow. We need to shop for flowers so we will have fresh petals to put in my flower girl basket.

There are so many colorful flowers to choose from—red and yellow and pink and orange. Mm-m-m! They smell so good!

Today's the day! We all get dressed in the dressing room. I'm glad I'm there because I can help Aunt Jessica with her veil.

She helps me, too.

One last look in the mirror. I'm a little nervous.
So is she.

"We'll both be just fine!" says Aunt Jessica. "I don't know what I'd do without you. I'm so glad you're my flower girl."

But when I see all the people
at the wedding looking at me,
I'm not so sure!

I turn around to see if Aunt Jessica
is watching. She gives me a "thumbs
up." That means "You can do it, Katy!"

The music plays.
Here I go! I walk slowly,
very slowly. I scatter my
flower petals as I go.
Mom, Dad, Grandma,
and all the guests smile
at me.

I smile, too. I like
being a flower girl!

Before I know it, I am all the way down the aisle. New music plays—*dum-dum-deedum*! Everyone turns around to look. Here comes the bride! She holds onto her dad's arm, tight. (Her dad is my grandpa!) I know how she feels. I give Aunt Jessica a thumbs up.

Soon Aunt Jessica and Ted are married.

They are husband and wife. And Ted is *Uncle* Ted.

The photographer takes lots of pictures for Aunt Jessica and Uncle Ted to put in their wedding album. The pictures will help them remember this day.

After the pictures are taken, we go inside for lunch. My cousin and I get a little silly at the table. Look! We can balance spoons on our noses!

Then the band begins. The bride and groom dance the first dance.

Soon everyone is dancing. Me, too. It feels good to
get up and move around—and have some fun!

But what we're really waiting for is dessert!
Isn't the wedding cake beautiful?
We count the layers —one, two, three, four!

Finally, it's time to cut the cake. Yum!

The fun isn't over yet though. Aunt Jessica and Uncle Ted have a surprise for me. What could it be?

It's a ring! A pretty ring of my very own!

"Thank you, Katy," they say. "Thank you for being our flower girl. You did a great job!"
And I know I did!